"Go Ahead, Karen," Someone Said . . .

I sat looking at the bottle in front of me. If it had been a tarantula I couldn't have been more scared of it. Where was all this wonderful confidence the book had promised me? I was supposed to be super-ready.

"So start, Karen," John said. "Give it a good spin."

Oh, help. I put my hand on the bottle and closed my eyes. Let it stop on Mark. If it doesn't, I'll die. Don't let it stop on Mark. If it does, I'll double die.

"Spin, spin," everyone called. Didn't *they* feel the way *I* felt? Wasn't anyone else terrified?

Books by Eve Bunting

GHOST BEHIND ME
STRANGE THINGS HAPPEN IN THE WOODS
KAREN KEPPLEWHITE IS THE WORLD'S BEST KISSER
MOTHER, HOW COULD YOU!

Available from ARCHWAY Paperbacks

Karen Kepplewhite is the World's Best Kisser

Eve Bunting

AN ARCHWAY PAPERBACK
Published by POCKET BOOKS
New York   London   Toronto   Sydney   Tokyo

This book is a work of fiction. Names, characters, places and incidents are either the product of the author's imagination or are used fictitiously. Any resemblance to actual events or locales or persons, living or dead, is entirely coincidental.

 An Archway Paperback published by
POCKET BOOKS, a division of Simon & Schuster Inc.
1230 Avenue of the Americas, New York, NY 10020

Published by arrangement with Clarion Books/Ticknor and Fields,
A Division of Houghton Mifflin Company
Library of Congress Catalog Card Number: 83-2066

ISBN: 0-671-63327-9

First Archway Paperback printing November 1984

10 9 8 7 6 5

AN ARCHWAY PAPERBACK and colophon are
registered trademarks of Simon & Schuster Inc.

Printed in the U.S.A.

IL 4+

To Gail and Lael
who loved KAREN from the beginning

Karen
Kepplewhite
is the World's
Best
Kisser

Chapter One

Mark Ritchie is not supposed to be the best-looking boy in the seventh grade. Most of the girls think John Hunt is cuter. And my best friend, Janet Hamm, says Danny DePuzo has a better bod. Janet is very big on bods.

But, oh, I like Mark. I'm not sure about his bod. I'm a bit shy and I don't really like to look. Besides, I'm not certain what I'd be looking for! But I do know about Mark's smile, and his eyes and his hair. They're all terrific. He's tall, too, and quiet. And I like quiet boys. And he's not one of the class dummies either, which to me is very important.

What's unbelievable is Mark's coming to my thirteenth birthday party on Saturday. I'm so jazzed I can hardly stand it.

Today in social studies, Janet passed me a note. I opened it under cover of my European history text. Janet was watching me with that sly look on her face that she sometimes gets.

The note said:

1

Dear Karen:
    I have a *big* surprise for you.

Janet always writes with half of the words underlined and the other half capitalized.

    It's a *secret* surprise and you must tell NO ONE. Last night, in the mall, Mom and I bought you a present. And THEN . . . I saw this *something* that you positively must have before your BIRTHDAY. It will dazzle M.

M, of course, is Mark. I looked over at Janet and she quickly pulled the corner of a red wrapped package from her book bag. Then she pushed it down again. What could it be? I had a feeling that Mark would be hard to dazzle. I went back to reading.

Be in the park at lunchtime. REMEMBER. Bring *no one*.

I folded up the note and put it in my purse. Janet! Janet! What IS it?
    As soon as the lunch bell rang I rushed out. Janet was already waiting and we left right away for the park.
    The park is across the street from school and everyone uses it at lunchtime and after. Some of the kids smoke in the rest rooms. The school tried putting the park off limits two or three times but

2

nobody paid any attention. In the end they just gave up. Now a parent patrol keeps an eye on it for perverts and things like that. Janet and I come here a lot but we've never seen a pervert yet.

Janet was carrying the book bag.

"You're going to DIE when you see this. Honest, Karen. It's the most FABULOUS THING."

Janet talks in capitals, the way she writes. I've gotten into the habit of watching the words come out of her mouth as if they're written in balloons, most of them underlined. People tell me that one of my best assets is the way I listen. I always look very intently at the person. I don't know if it is an asset, though. Once a lady in a store began shouting at me and I discovered that she thought I was deaf and lip-reading.

Janet and I were waiting at the crosswalk for the light to change when someone called. It was Francine Grady and a couple of other girls.

"Hey, you two! Wait up!" Francine yelled. "Are you going to eat in the park?"

"Yes," Janet said. "But we have something VERY SECRET to discuss. No offense."

Janet believes in being up front about everything, so mostly she tacks "no offense" on to soften the blow.

"It's about the party," I told Francine and the others. It was lucky they were all invited. "We're planning a . . . surprise. You'll find out what it is on Saturday."

"I wouldn't be too SURE about them *finding out*,"

3

Janet said. *"Some people* will know something's different right away. But I'll bet *they* won't." She smiled mysteriously.

Francine shrugged. "Well, I guess we'll have to live without knowing."

The light had gone from red to green and Janet tugged me across the street. She carried the book bag between us and I could feel it bumping my legs. What could be in it?

I headed for our usual bench.

"Not there," Janet said impatiently. "ANYBODY could see or hear. Under the trees. Back in the corner."

There was bird gook on the bench under the trees. We wiped it off with our lunch napkins and sat down. Janet put the bag between us.

Some of the boys had drifted over to play softball. I saw Mark and my heart did its usual flip-flop. He was wearing cords and a blue knit shirt with a honey bear on the pocket. I wished I were the honey bear, right next to his heart. His bod looked wonderful.

"I'd DIE if they saw," Janet breathed.

I don't know why she was worried. Those boys hardly ever look at us unless they have to. Why would today be different?

"I think we're safe," I said. "Janet? Please tell me what's in the package!"

Slowly, mysteriously, Janet pulled it from the book bag. I had a feeling that what was in that package might change my entire life.

4

Chapter Two

Janet is a very dramatic person. I think that's why she talks and writes in capitals. I could tell by the way she held the package that we weren't going to get to it right away.

"What happened was this," she said.

I leaned forward to watch her mouth so I wouldn't miss anything.

"Mom and I went to Macy's in the mall. We got something for you. You'll like it OK. You'll probably like it a LOT. It's blue, with a zipper "

"Go on! Go on!" I begged.

"And you keep things in it."

"I don't mean go on about *that!*"

Janet turned the red package in her hand. "And then I found THIS. It's something *very special.*"

"I am dying," I said.

"It's from ME to YOU."

I was getting mad. Janet loves to pull this kind of

thing. I opened my lunch sack and pretended to be interested in my sandwich.

Janet put the package on my knees. "Here."

I jammed the sandwich back in the sack and pulled the red paper from the package. Inside was a book with a plain, brown cover. No title.

"What the heck . . .?" I began.

"Sh!" Janet covered the book with her hands as if to hide it from the eyes of a million spies, though there was no one to see. Except maybe the blue jay in the branch above us.

"*I* put the cover on," she whispered. "So no one would see what you're reading. Go ahead. Open it."

Inside it said: Do You WANT TO KNOW HOW TO KISS? EXPERTLY? SOULFULLY? SEXILY? *Everything you need to know is here in this book. Diagrams too. Not only is this a "how to." It is also a "when to" and a "where to."*

I don't know about Mark being dazzled. But I certainly was.

"Well?" Janet prodded me. "Isn't it SUPER? You'll be having *kissing* games at your party. Everybody else is going to be a *bummer* at it. EVERYBODY, except us."

I found my voice. "Us?"

"You and ME. This Wednesday. That gives us three nights to practice. We'll be *so* expert, soulful, and sexy."

I opened the book somewhere around the middle.

" 'Keep your lips parted,' " the book said.

6

" 'Tilt your head a little so the noses don't bump. Close your eyes, if you want to. Some gals and guys enjoy looking while they kiss. It's up to you. Don't press your lips too softly against his. He needs to know you're there. But don't push too hard either. Especially if either of you has braces!' " I frowned and read on.

" 'You'll want to put your arms around his neck, of course.' "

"Of course," I whispered.

" 'This brings a feeling of closeness,' " the book said. " 'And it's fine to let your fingers linger on his neck. He'll love it.' "

I closed the book fast. Let my fingers linger on his neck! Oh, help! Oh, heaven!

Janet's breathing was as loud as the pump at the school pool.

I jumped up, put the book under me and sat on it.

"Karen! You don't have to HIDE it. Nobody knows what it is but *us*."

"Janet Hamm! How could you buy such a thing? Didn't you die when you were paying for it? Was it a guy at the checkout? How did you have the nerve?"

"Why should I care?" Janet said. "I didn't even know him." She pushed at me. "Get up. You'll *wrinkle* it. This is our ticket—mine to Danny De-Puzo, yours to Mark Ritchie. We're going to be THE BEST KISSERS AROUND. Here, wait! I want to read you something."

7

I eased up and she squeezed the book out. "I checked this last night in bed. Just listen, Karen." She had a page turned down on the corner. In fact, I saw she had a bunch of corners turned down. I didn't get it. Wasn't this supposed to be *my* birthday present?

Janet read aloud and I peered over her shoulder.

" 'You may not be fabulous looking . . .' " She lifted her head. "And you're NOT, Karen. No offense."

"You're not exactly the model type yourself," I said.

Janet was reading again. " 'You may not have a great personality or a sharp sense of humor.' "

She looked at me and I waited for another "no offense" remark.

"You don't need to stop and tell me what I don't have on every line," I said. "Just read." I have to say that a friend who is up front doesn't do much for your self-confidence.

" 'You may not be a super dancer. Or a hotshot on the tennis court.' "

Aha! I waited for her to give me another of her sly little looks. Because, this time I had her. I'd won the junior all-league tennis match and also the round robin this year. And Janet is hopeless. I can wallop her at everything. Tennis, volleyball, softball. Especially tennis. But Janet wasn't about to stop and give me an opening.

" 'These things don't matter in the long run,' " she read. And now she stopped. "See? Just because

8

you're *good* at that stuff doesn't matter in the long run. It says SO RIGHT HERE." She was reading again. " 'Being a great kisser is what matters to the opposite sex. Learn to kiss well and you'll always be popular. Master the methods and you'll know them for life.' "

"I guess it's like riding a bicycle," I said. "Once you learn how, you never forget."

Janet nodded. She held the closed book on her knees with her hands crossed over it. It could have been some kind of religious work.

"And you know what I figure?" she said. "If you START doing it wrong, you'll always do it wrong. Like all bad habits."

That made sense. "Like typing with only four fingers," I said.

"Or holding the Ping-Pong paddle *wrong*," Janet added.

She should know about that one.

I looked down at the book. "What I don't understand is what else is in here? One page ought to be able to tell you how to kiss. It can't be that hard. Everybody does it."

"Everybody but *us*," Janet reminded me.

I ignored that. "One page. And I think I just read that page. All about lips and noses and fingers wandering over his neck."

I swallowed and glanced across the wet grass. It was easy for me to find Mark in his blue shirt. Face it, it would have been easy for me to find him anywhere, any time. "Kissing seems so simple," I

9

said weakly. "It's just finding someone who wants to kiss. Someone you want to kiss back."

"You didn't think it was so SIMPLE at Francine Grady's party," Janet said. "You said it was AWFUL. And *Danny* said you were AWFUL too." She put her hand over her mouth. "Oops!"

"Danny DePuzo told you I kiss awful?"

"Well, you burped, he said. Just when he was leaning toward you."

"I couldn't help it. I was nervous. Besides, I think it was very rude of Danny DePuzo to complain. I think that shows the kind of person he is."

Janet sighed. "You don't understand Danny. And you were only nervous because you DIDN'T KNOW HOW TO DO IT." She was so enthusiastic now I thought her word balloon might burst. I imagined all the sentences scattering on the grass. She patted the book. "No more nervous. Read *this* and you'll know EVERYTHING."

I didn't have the courage to tell Janet. But I had to. "I wasn't planning on having any kissing games at my party," I said. "I think it's dumb, if you want to know. Kissing all those boys you don't want to kiss in the first place." And scary, I thought. Super scary.

Janet leaped off the bench all aquiver. Janet is a little plump, especially in the cheeks, which are of the semi-chipmunk variety. No offense. When she's all aquiver she really is.

"You're having DANNY and MARK and that foxy John Hunt! And Michael Moss, who ain't bad

10

either! And you're not planning on any *kissing games?* You've got to be crazy!"

I was a bit aquiver myself. "I don't think any of the kids really like it." And I wanted the party to be a success. Didn't Janet understand that?

"Don't LIKE it? You *are* crazy. Why do you think they're coming? All those boys? We're not a bunch of babies, you know? Nobody likes *little goodie-goodie* parties. You never told me you WEREN'T . . ."

She stopped and looked at me. "OK. I'll tell you something. I'm not *supposed* to, but I *will* anyway. Danny told ME that Mark told HIM that THAT was why he was coming to your party."

My heart was going plumpity-plump. "Because of the kissing games?" Good grief! Who did he want to kiss? Or should that be "whom" did he want to kiss?

"That's right," Janet said grimly. "But do what you want. It's your party."

Across the grass, I saw Mark. He was standing in a backward sort of curve, and his arm was raised to throw a ball. I thought about the back of his neck. I couldn't see it, of course, but I imagined it all smooth and brown.

I closed my eyes and began stroking the bench. And right away I got a splinter in my finger, big as a shark's tooth. Which shows how dumb it is to let your fingers linger on a crummy old park bench.

"OK," I said. "We'll have kissing games."

What was I letting myself in for?

11

Chapter Three

Janet was coming over to my house at eight so we could practice. And I don't mean the violin! By that time I'd have had supper, done my homework, and visited Gran.

Gran lives in an apartment three doors from us, which is very nice for everyone. Her name is Kepplewhite, too, because she's Dad's mother. And she is wonderful. I can tell her anything and she listens. I mean, she just sits, without doing anything else and listens.

I can tell my mom most things too. But usually she only semi-listens. She's scraping carrots at the same time, or folding laundry, or one hand's writing the grocery list while the other's paying bills. Mom's a dental hygienist and she works four and a half days a week. So she's always busy. Actually, it's pretty neat of her to let me have this party. There's going to be lots of food and she and Gran and Dad and I are making every bit of it.

I got to Gran's in time for *Leave It to Beaver*. That's our favorite program. They're all reruns and Gran says Wally and Beaver are pretty old now, not kids at all. The shows are great, though—especially the one we saw tonight. It was all about Wally going on a date with a girl and borrowing his dad's car the way he always does. He begs for it! And then Beaver got in the back seat, accidentally, and fell asleep. So Wally and the girl park up at Lover's Lane and then they find dumb little Beaver all curled up and cute. Except Wally doesn't think he's cute.

It's neat how they always have places like Make-out Point or Lovers' Lane in old TV programs. I guess in those days they built special places for stuff like that. I don't think they do anymore.

When *Beaver* was over we switched off the TV to talk. I told Gran about the book.

"Did you bring it?" she asked. "I'd like to have a look at that. You're never too old to learn, you know."

"I'll bring it tomorrow if you like."

Gran had set out a platter of big black grapes and some thin slices of white cheese. That's the kind of dessert we always have at her house. Gran's not a real great cook. She never bakes cookies or cakes or pies. She says when it got fashionable to be healthy, she came into her own.

I took a grape, squished it in my mouth, and spat out the seeds while Gran went to get our Rubik's

Cubes. We each have one and we're in strong competition to see who can solve it first. We've been working on them for a long time.

Gran says Rubik's Cubes are about as out of date now as *Leave It to Beaver*. But, like Beaver, they're still fun. We keep ours in one of Gran's cupboards in two paper sacks. Each night we seal off the sacks with Gran's sealing wax. Then I take the wax home. That's so Gran won't cheat and work on hers when I'm not there.

"You know," Gran said when she came back with the cubes, "I'm surprised. I always thought kissing came naturally. But I suppose there's always room for science."

We sat on the couch, side by side, clicking and shifting our cubes. Gran's is in every mixed-up combination possible. It looks worse than when she started.

"Janet says knowing how to be great kissers will make us super-popular. She says it's the way to a boy's heart."

Gran laughed. She laughs a lot at the things Janet says. And sometimes she shakes her head and remarks, "Oh, that Janet!" I'm not sure how she really feels about her.

"When I was young they said the way to a man's heart was through his stomach," Gran said now. "And since I was a rotten cook that made me very nervous." She closed her eyes, gave her cube a vicious twist, squinted at it, and said, "Darn!"

"Was it?" I asked. "The way to his heart?"

"You mean through his stomach? No. That was baloney. But in those days I didn't know any better."

"You mean, you didn't know that being a great kisser was the way?"

"No. That's baloney too." Gran's fingers stopped moving on the cube. "You don't set out to do something like that. You just be yourself. And you make yourself somebody worthwhile. Interesting. Independent. Then you'll find the way to each other's heart just comes naturally."

"But being a great kisser couldn't hurt," I said.

Gran leaned forward and touched my cheek. "Probably not. But keep those other things in mind, too, Karen."

Just then the doorbell rang. Gran put her cube down. "No fair working on yours while I'm gone," she warned.

I made myself a grape and cheese sandwich while I waited. That would be the end of talking for tonight. Gran has all kinds of friends who stop by to gab and drink celery juice. I wondered which one this was.

"Hello, Star," I heard Gran say. "You're just in time to meet Karen, my granddaughter. I told you about her yesterday. Come on in."

"Are you sure it's OK? I won't be in the way?"

I sat up straight. A girl voice. A girl-about-my-age voice.

"Sure, I'm sure," Gran said. "It's perfect. In fact, I should have asked you to come."

15

I stood up.

"Karen? This is Star Sumner. She and her mother have just moved into the apartment behind me. Star, Karen Kepplewhite."

I stared. For a minute I thought Gran had said Star Sumptuous. And it wouldn't have been far off. Sumptuous violet eyes. Sumptuous blonde hair that hung loose on one side and dangled in a little braid on the other. I wondered if my hair was long enough to fix like that.

Star wore blue walking shorts, a blue shirt—all neatly ironed—white knee socks and leather top-siders. I knew it was the new "fresh" look, though nobody at my school was into it yet.

"Hi!" Star showed perfect teeth and perfect dimples when she smiled.

"Sit down," Gran said. "Have a piece of cheese. Have a grape. Have a Rubik's Cube." I hoped she was joking about the cube.

Star sat on the other side of the couch from me. "Rubik's Cubes are great, aren't they? How long does it take you to solve one?"

"About a lifetime, I expect," Gran said cheerfully. "You mean those things are solvable?"

Star dimpled. "Well, I'm not a real expert. It takes me about a half hour. Some of the kids in my school could do it in five minutes. One boy could do it with his toes." Star made a move to take Gran's cube from her. "You want me to show you?"

Gran held it tight to her chest. "No, no. Don't

16

touch. Karen and I are in strict competition. There's a trip to Disneyland riding on this."

I eyed Gran suspiciously. "And the same goes if Star's here and I'm not. No cheating."

Gran laughed. "She certainly does trust her sweet old grandmother! Let's put the cubes away and talk."

Star watched as we secured the bags and put them in the refrigerator. She watched me pocket the wax.

"You sure do take it seriously, don't you?"

"You betcha." Gran passed the grapes. "Star's going to start in Washington Junior High after spring vacation," she told me. George Washington is the school I go to.

Star bit a grape daintily in half. "Your grandmother says we'll be in the same grade." I'd never seen anybody bite a grape like that without making a mess. "I'm so glad I'll know at least somebody there. It's pretty scary, starting in a new school."

I nodded. The way Star looked, she needn't worry. Everybody would be tripping out, trying to meet her. I could imagine Danny DePuzo. You could bet he wouldn't miss Star.

Once, when I was walking home from school after girls' health ed, Danny came up to me on his bicycle.

"Hi, Karen," he said. "How are your Fallopian tubes today?"

Fallopian tubes are things women have inside

17

them. They're part of the reproductive system, but I'd never heard of them myself until that day. That Danny DePuzo knows everything!

He was grinning away at me from his bicycle. "Well, how are the old tubes?"

"Fine," I said. "And how are yours?" I hurried on before Danny could say anything more.

I never did tell Janet about Danny and my tubes. Some things are not worth repeating. However, this is the kind of boy Danny DePuzo is. He'll notice Star all right. And Mark? I tried not to think about him.

"It's too bad there's no chance for Star to meet a few of the other kids too," Gran said. "I mean, before school starts."

Gran's too cool to come right out with it. She'd never say, Why don't you invite her to your birthday party?

No way, Gran, I thought. I don't want to invite her. And I have my reasons. I took another grape and said nothing.

"Where did you move from, Star?" I asked at last.

"San Francisco."

"Did your dad get transferred or something?" It seemed the only kind of reason anyone would move from that wonderful city.

Star lowered her head. "No. My dad died . . . last year. Mom's two sisters live here. So we came. I think Mom's been pretty lonely."

Her dad died. My stomach suddenly hurt. I guess

18

I'd eaten too many grapes. How awful to have your dad die! One minute he'd be around, calling you "kiddo" the way my dad always does. Maybe he'd be grumping because I'd messed up his morning paper. And then, wham! He'd be gone! I could hardly look at Star. I swallowed and I don't know what happened. The words just came popping right out of my mouth.

"I'm having a birthday party on Saturday. A lot of the seventh-grade kids will be there. Would you like to come?"

Star smiled. "Oh, Karen. I'd love to."

Gran smiled too.

I sat back. Well, I'd done it. Star was coming. I suppose I'd been nice to ask her. I had a strong feeling that I'd also been stupid.

Chapter Four

Dad and my little brother, Georgie, were playing robot when I got home. I think they were supposed to be the two guys from one of those old space movies. And they were the right shape. Georgie is small and round, Dad is tall and thin.

Georgie is always playing at being someone from another planet. Usually he's Superman. Tonight, though, he had a paper bag over his head. Dad did too. They had holes cut out for eyes and mouths.

"Hi, kiddo," Dad said.

"Hi." I stood looking at him, feeling all kinds of hurts inside. Suppose he were the one who'd died?

"Robots don't say, 'Hi, kiddo,' " Georgie objected. "Say something else, Robot D."

Before Dad could answer I rushed at him. I threw my arms around his waist and hugged him tight. "Oh, Dad," I whispered, somewhere against his middle.

Dad pulled off the paper bag. "Sweetie! What's the matter?"

"Nothing. I love you, that's all."

"Well, I love you too."

I turned and ran up the stairs. Behind me I could hear Georgie complaining. "Robots don't say 'Sweetie.' You keep forgetting to talk like a robot, Dad. Put your head back on."

I went in the bathroom to blow my nose and wash my face. I never used to cry this easily. Mom says it's part of being almost thirteen, but I'm not sure what that has to do with it. I combed my hair. While I was at it I fixed it in a little braid down one side like you-know-who's. Just to cheer me up. It looked pretty cute, and I did feel better.

When I opened the door for Janet the first thing she said was, "Ugh! What have you done to your hair? It looks awful. No offense."

"Maybe it's too short," I muttered. "Or too curly."

"Your hair is gorgeous, you big dummo. Why are you messing with it? I just wish I had hair like yours."

One thing I have to say for Janet. She can be up front nice as well as up front not so nice. I guess that's one of the reasons I like her.

She couldn't believe it when I told her about Star. We were sitting on the floor of my room with the book between us.

"How could you *do* it?" Janet asked. "Someone

who looks like THAT! And after we planned so *carefully*." She stopped and we looked away from each other. I knew what she meant about our careful planning. And I wasn't exactly proud of it either.

Neither one of us had ever come right out and said it, but we knew all right. What we had done was not invite any of the really terrific girls in the seventh grade to my party. The six we aren't dogs, or anything like that. They're just not what Danny DePuzo calls "the class babes." Janet and I and the rest are—well, sort of middle class.

"Look," I said. "Star's new and her dad died last year. What do you expect me to do?" I didn't add, Besides, my Gran was right there. But I knew that had a lot to do with it. Is it a crime to want your grandmother to think you're a nice person?

Janet spread her hands. "*I* don't have a dad either. And I don't see anyone asking ME to parties just for that reason."

"Look," I said. "It's different with you. Your mom and dad are just divorced. That's not the same as dead. And you see him all the time."

"Well, you didn't make HER dad die. What makes *you* responsible for her? And you know what you've got now, don't you?"

I nodded. "Thirteen. That's an unlucky number."

"You've got six boys and seven girls. That's a *real* unlucky number. Especially if *one* of the girls is TOTALLY AWESOME."

"She won't have read the book," I said.

"Doesn't the book say that looks don't count? What counts is being a super kisser?"

Janet bit her lip. "With *her* looks she's probably had lots of REAL, LIVE EXPERIENCE."

"Probably," I said. "Read, Janet. Now more than ever we need the book."

Janet read. "Ways to get to know the boy of your dreams."

"Maybe we should skip that," I suggested. "We know them already."

Janet hunched over the book. "No. There's good stuff here. Listen. 'A smile is very productive. A smile says, I like you—I want to get to know you better.'" She stopped and stared into space. "I think maybe I don't SMILE enough," she said at last and went back to reading. "'A smile says, Why don't you ask me out? We could have fun together.'"

Janet's chipmunk cheeks were rosy red. "Did you *know* a smile could say ALL THAT? We've been walking around, not SMILING enough, and doing ourselves in. Boy, from now on I'm gonna smile *so hard* at Danny DePuzo he'll think I'm the most fun person around."

"I hope he doesn't think you're bananas."

Janet sniffed. "Don't be so negative, Karen. 'Winking is a good approach,'" she read. "'A wink says, I really dig you. I think you're the tops.'"

"The tops?" I asked.

23

"This is *great* advice," Janet said. "I didn't KNOW about winking either."

She was so jazzed up that I felt myself being carried along too. Tomorrow I'd go up to Mark and smile. I might even wink. But I wouldn't try them both at the same time. I gave a small practice flick of my eyelid and saw Janet do the same.

" 'Giggling can really turn a guy on,' " she continued. " 'He thinks it's cute and feminine. But don't go too far. He could think you're laughing at him. And that's not a turn-on . . . that's a turn-off.' "

"I should think so," I agreed.

Janet closed the book. "Maybe we should concentrate on *this* before we go any further."

"You mean, practice smiling, winking, and giggling? I don't think we need to. We can handle that. Let's move on to the more advanced stuff."

Janet flipped a few pages. "The next part is on being a good talker. 'There are several good ways to start a conversation. You can ask, What school do you go to?' "

We began giggling for real then.

"What *school* do you go to?"

"They'd really think we'd flipped!"

Georgie opened the door. "What are you guys laughing about?"

Janet quickly put the book behind her back.

"Get lost, Georgie," I told him. "And you know you're supposed to knock."

We went through the rest of the chapter.

There were all kinds of hints on good conversation. " 'Know what his interests are?' " Janet read. "I wonder what DANNY's interests are."

"Girls," I said.

Janet nodded. "This girl, Star? She was *really* terrific, huh, Karen?" Janet sounded very cool, but I could tell she was wishing Star wouldn't be at my party. And to tell the truth, I was wishing it too. Who needed that kind of competition?

"Do you think she's Danny's *type*? Tell me honestly, Karen."

"Well, I don't know." I happen to think anyone with Fallopian tubes is Danny's type. But I wasn't going to tell Janet that. Star was probably Mark's type too and he'd pick her for all the kissing games and I'd die.

"Are you sure we should have kissing games?" I asked and Janet looked at me as if I'd gone mad. She sighed and I sighed and for a few seconds we had a duet going. Life isn't always easy.

Janet had to be home by ten, so at a quarter of we called it quits.

"Who gets the book overnight?" Janet asked.

"I do," I said. "It's my book."

"*I* bought it. And anyway, it's not your birthday *yet*. I'm not going to give it to you till your birthday."

"You already gave it to me."

Janet fondled the cover. "I don't think it's fair if you get to work on it more than I do. One of us shouldn't end up being a *better kisser* than the other one." We were beginning to sound like Gran and me with the Rubik's Cubes.

"I'll only read a little," I promised. "And tomorrow night you can take it home." I'm really a very good friend.

So we agreed on that. We agreed, too, that in school tomorrow we'd start up some conversations with boys. Not only with Mark and Danny. We decided to practice on some lesser types first. We would also smile, wink, and giggle a lot. But not so much that we'd look spaced out.

"We'll use our common sense," Janet said.

We shook hands on it. I don't think Janet and I ever shook hands on anything before, which shows how serious we were.

I stayed in my room after she left and picked up the book where we'd left off. I studied every illustration, right side up and upside down. Sideways too, in case I missed anything.

I knew I'd promised to read only a little. But this book was like peanuts. There was no way to stop once I'd started. Besides, I was sure Janet would be reading tomorrow night till her eyeballs hurt.

Mom came in to ask if I was OK. She's not used to me staying in my room the whole night.

"Sure, I'm OK." I hid the book under the covers. "I'm just reading."

Mom dumped the pile of clothes off my chair and sat. "Did you brush your teeth, honey?"

I nodded. I swear my mother has asked me that question every night of my life. She probably even asked me when I was a baby and had no teeth. She used to make me open my mouth for inspection, but thank heavens she's stopped that. I knew what was coming next.

"Floss 'em good?"

I nodded again. I think it comes from her being a dental hygienist. She brings her work home.

"Well," she said. "Just three days till your birthday. Are you excited?"

I squished down, the book jabbing against my side. "I sure am." And I thought, I'm scared too.

I'd told Mom about Star and she'd said it was nice of me to ask her. Now she said, "One table will have five sitting at it, not four. But that shouldn't be a problem."

Three girls and two boys? That could be a problem all right. But I didn't say anything. Besides, I'd had a wonderful idea about the tables. I squished down farther.

Mom bent down and kissed my cheek. "Don't read too long, honey bun."

"I won't. Good night."

I lay and thought about the party, of course. I decided we should have only two or three kissing games. We didn't want to look too grabby. And what about my new idea for the tables? Oh, man! Scary wasn't the word for this.

I took out the book again.

" 'If you want to nibble on his ear, go right ahead. He'll enjoy it. This would be a good time to say, Your hair smells so nice, and it's so soft.' "

27

I kicked off the sheet. Saying that! And nibbling on his ear! Ears seemed so private. Would Mark really like to have his nibbled? I couldn't imagine doing it—it seemed almost gross. Maybe there were things in this book that you had to work up to.

" 'Some guys enjoy having their arms stroked. You can start with hand holding. Let your fingers move up and stroke the inside of his arm, gently, tenderly.' "

I kicked the sheet all the way onto the floor. I'd NEVER be able to do these things. But maybe, by the time Saturday came . . .

I turned to the chapter on "Confidence."

" 'Before you go to sleep each night say to yourself, I am the world's best kisser. If you like, you can put your own name in. This sends the message deeper into your subconscious.' "

I pulled up the sheet and switched off the lamp. Then I said out loud, "Karen Kepplewhite is the world's best kisser. Karen Kepplewhite is the world's best kisser."

I hoped my subconscious was getting the message.

Chapter Five

Janet and I giggled and smiled a lot the next day.

Danny DePuzo came up as we were giggling in the corridor.

"What school do you go to, Danny?" Janet asked, and then we giggled for real.

"You two are definitely weird," Danny said and walked away.

We wiped our eyes.

While Mrs. Waters, my English teacher, discussed *The Legend of Sleepy Hollow* I stared at the back of Mark's neck. I dreamed about fingers that did the walking . . . and I don't mean through the Yellow Pages.

Maybe Mark felt my imagination crawling on him like an itsy-bitsy spider. Anyway, he turned and gave me one of his vague looks. To be truthful, that's about the only kind I ever got from him. They make me instant mush.

I gathered myself together and winked. My heart

was pumping. It was a perfect wink that plainly said, I really dig you. I think you're the tops.

Mark yawned. He scratched under his left armpit and turned away.

I decided you have to be real close to someone, vis-à-vis, as Mrs. Waters would say, to get the effect of a wink. Vis-à-vis is French for face to face.

I also decided that there aren't many guys who could look cute while scratching under an armpit. Mark just happens to be one of them.

At lunchtime a boy named Simon Wuhlfeiler sat at our table. He's a brain and kind of quiet.

I took a deep breath.

"I hear they caught one of those dangerous fruit flies in a trap in L.A.," I said. "I hope that doesn't mean trouble."

Simon went on munching his tuna surprise.

Janet dug her elbow in my side and made a circle with her thumb and forefinger. That meant I was doing good.

"I hope we don't get worms in our apples, and stuff," I said. "Maggots."

Simon spooned up the last of his noodles. "It's not a subject I care to discuss over lunch." He gathered up his books and left.

"Shoot!" I said. "*I* thought that was pretty interesting. *My mom* thought it was pretty interesting this morning. Dad read it to her from the paper. At breakfast too. It didn't seem to bother her."

"I thought it was VERY interesting," Janet agreed. "Simon Wuhlfeiler is a total toad."

I cheered up when I tried the fruit fly bit on John Hunt. He looked interested right away. "Oh, yeah? How do they trap them?" he asked.

"Uh . . . uh . . ."

"Maybe it's one of those jaw traps, with teeth," he said. "It catches the legs. They use them with wolves and bears."

"Maybe." I got away fast.

Janet and I walked home together.

"There's one thing," I said. "If you start an interesting conversation you should know how to follow up on it. They ought to add that to the book."

"I know," Janet said. "Let's write afterwards and let the book people know what *works* and what *doesn't*."

"Oh, let's!"

I told her about my idea for the tables, which was to have place cards with everyone's name written on them. She thought it was a terrific idea. Which it was.

"That way, we can arrange who we'll sit beside," I said.

Janet nudged me. "And *we* know WHO."

We sure did.

Janet had to go to her piano lesson at four.

"I have to fix a meat loaf for dinner anyway," I said. "Why don't you come over about eight?"

"Unless you'd rather come to my house," Janet offered.

"No. You come to mine." I really don't like going to Janet's. Her mother doesn't "work outside the home" as the game-show hosts always say. The problem is, she doesn't work inside the home either. She sits around a lot drinking coffee. The house is always messy, and to tell the truth, so is Mrs. Hamm. She doesn't seem to pay much attention to Janet or to Janet's big brother, Wilmer, either.

I didn't know Janet before the divorce, which was four years ago, so it's hard to tell if it was the same mess that drove Mr. Hamm away or if the mess came after.

Now Janet and I went our separate ways.

Mom had left the ground round out to defrost and I chopped onion and mixed the meat with bread crumbs and Worcestershire sauce and a can of tomato soup, which is the way we like our meat loaf. Oh, yes, and beaten-up egg. I scrubbed potatoes for baking. Then I checked to see that there was everything for a salad.

I was just wondering if I should go upstairs and read the book again when the phone rang.

The minute I picked it up I recognized the voice.

"Karen? This is Star."

"Oh, hi."

"I hope you don't mind me calling. Your grandmother gave me your number."

"It's fine."

"I'm just about to walk to Trimble's for a malt," Star said. "The trouble with not being in school is it gets boring, you know?"

"I guess. It doesn't sound too boring to me."

"You only think that till it happens. TV is awful in the daytime, unless you like those silly soaps. And I don't."

"It's not so great in the evening either, except for *Leave It to Beaver.*"

"I've been reading a bunch of books."

"Oh, what?"

Star paused. "Well, *Wuthering Heights* for about the tenth time. And *Rebecca*. And a bunch of science fiction stuff." She paused again. "And romances. But *Wuthering Heights* is my favorite."

"I know," I said. "Heathcliff."

We seemed to have run out of things to talk about.

"I don't suppose you'd like to walk to Trimble's with me?" Star's voice sounded kind of shy. "I mean, if you're not busy with homework or something."

"I've only got math and I can do it later. I'd really like to come. Banana coconut is their flavor of the week. Do you want to come by here?"

"Great." Star sounded pleased. "See you in a few minutes."

I wrote a quick note for Dad telling him where I was, and when to put the meat loaf and potatoes in the oven. He picks Georgie up from day care and gets in about five.

Then I ran upstairs and changed into my new jeans and my "It's-a-Dilly" T-shirt. The jeans aren't the kind with someone's name written across the butt, but they look good. I didn't know why I cared so much how I was dressed today, but I did. It had to do with Star and knowing she'd be looking great without even trying. I brushed my hair and decided not to go for the side braid.

Needless to say, when I saw Star I was glad I'd fixed myself up. She was wearing pink culottes and a pink polo shirt with white knee socks. I decided knee socks must be "in" in San Francisco. Her hair was plain and straight, with just one barrette on the left side. I decided one barrette must be the style there, too. The polo shirt was semi-tight and I noticed right away that Star was pretty flat in front. I felt good about that, since I'm pretty flat myself.

"Hi," Star said.

"Hi."

We walked down Lake Avenue past all the little boutiques and jewelry shops, and I discovered that until you know a person really well, you just walk. You don't stop to talk about the stuff in the windows and if it'd look good on you or not.

"Do you think you're going to like it here?" I asked.

"I don't know. It's hard leaving all your friends."

I changed my shoulder purse from my right shoulder to my left so we wouldn't keep bumping. "Is your name really Star? Or is that short for something?"

"It's really Star. The night before I was born, my mom and dad were standing outside in our backyard. There was this huge, bright star in the sky. My

34

dad said it was the brightest star he'd ever seen in his life. They decided the baby would be named Star." She shrugged. "Good thing I wasn't a boy, I guess."

"That's romantic," I said. "Maybe it wasn't a star at all, since it was so bright. Maybe it was a comet, or a meteor."

Star giggled. "Thank heavens they didn't call me Comet. I'd remind people of a bathroom cleanser."

I giggled too. After a minute I said, "Was your dad killed in an accident? I hope you don't mind me asking."

"That's OK. No, he just died. He was sick for a long time."

"Oh." I thought it was really sad. The little baby, Star, and the father and all. I know she wasn't a baby when he died, but still. He must have loved her a lot. I had a giant-sized lump in my throat and I felt like stopping right then and hugging her. But she'd have thought me a space case.

"My mom's working already," Star said. "She's a nurse, and she got a job in the community hospital."

"Hey!" I smiled. "That was fast! My mom's a sort of nurse too. She's a dental hygienist."

"No kidding?" Star smiled back and I felt pretty good. It was as if we had something in common. Then she said the most incredible thing: "That's probably why you have such terrific teeth. I noticed them first thing."

"You did?" I ran my tongue across them. Imagine! All that brushing and flossing must have paid off.

We were almost at Trimble's now on the corner of Lake and California. I could see its pretty red-and-white-striped awnings.

"I guess you have a Trimble's in San Francisco too. . . ." I began, and stopped. Three boys stood in front of Brown's Book Store, right next to Trimble's. They had their backs to us as they looked in Brown's window. I'd have known one of those backs anywhere. Actually, I'd have known all three of them.

Danny DePuzo of the great bod. John Hunt, who's supposed to be the best-looking guy in the seventh grade, although he bites his nails really badly. (John is coming to my party too; you can see that Janet and I didn't just ask the middle-class boys!) The third, and definitely most adorable back of all, belonged to Mark.

Oh, no! I could tell that any minute now the boys were going to turn around. What would happen when they saw Star?

Chapter Six

"**O**h, oh." I felt my face get red. It always does at the prospect of a vis-à-vis with Mark.

"What's the matter?" Star asked.

"Those three boys are from school." We were so close behind them now that I could hear Danny giggling. His giggle, however, did *not* sound cute. These giggles wouldn't turn anyone on; they were plain old nasty.

Then Danny said something in a fake, squeaky voice.

"Oh, look, Mary Lou! I've just got to have that book. *How to Kiss Like an Expert*. Oh, it's just what I've always needed."

I froze. I knew who Mary Lou was. Danny meant Mary Lou Smith, who is definitely not the most popular girl in the seventh grade. Danny was probably imitating Betsy Sanchez, Mary Lou's best friend. How mean! That Danny DePuzo is definitely a mean guy. How can Janet like him? I thanked heaven a million times that Danny didn't know she and I had *How to Kiss Like an Expert*.

In the space between Mark's shoulder and Danny's head I could see Brown's window display. It was totally filled with the kissing book. A few copies dangled from red ribbons, others were propped against vases of red plastic roses. Some copies were open. I could see the very diagrams I'd studied so closely last night. Horror upon horrors!

"You don't think anybody would actually be dumb enough to buy that book?" John asked.

"There couldn't be anybody that dumb," Mark said, and I was standing behind, shaking my head. Of course not. Me? Don't be so silly. You think I'm that dumb?

It was just at that second that Mark turned and saw Star and me.

I pretended to swat at a fly.

"Hi," Mark said.

Then all three of them had turned toward us.

"Hi." It's funny how I have trouble looking at Mark. It's as if he's the sun, or something. I concentrated on Danny.

"Hi, Karen." I guess Danny was supposed to be speaking to me. Bur for sure he wasn't looking at me. He was eyeballing Star.

"Hi." John jerked a thumb over his shoulder at the window. "Were you just on your way in to buy one of these, Karen? Don't let us stop you."

I felt my face getting redder than ever. "Honestly, John Hunt! You must think I'm crazy. I wouldn't be caught dead buying that book." True. "I wouldn't buy it even if . . . even if . . ." I couldn't think of a way to finish the sentence.

Danny helped me. "Even if you weren't an expert kisser already. Which, of course, you are." He gave another silly cackle. What a yuk! Janet must be crazy, no question.

"I wouldn't say you're such a wonderful kisser yourself," I began and then realized that nobody was listening. When Star was around, probably no one ever listened.

"Who's your friend?" Danny asked. Danny's the kind who would put it like that, sort of smart-alecky. I think he picks things up from old TV movies.

"This is Star Sumner. She's going to Washington after spring break. She'll be in seventh grade too."

"Hey, great!" All three boys grinned like hyenas. Even Mark. But, of course, Mark is very polite.

"That's Mark. That's John and that's Danny," I told Star.

Star smiled. She bobbed her head and the side of hair that hung free swung forward, all gleaming and golden. It seemed to stun the three of them. Dazzled them, I thought, and she hadn't done a thing except be herself—bright, white, gleaming Star.

I looked secretly at Mark. He was as agog as the other two. I should be smiling myself—giggling, winking, anything. I felt numb. The book would have been ashamed of me.

"Are you going in to Trimble's?" John asked and I nodded.

"Us too." Danny had wormed himself over next to Star. "What are you going to have?"

I looked up and saw Mark holding the door open for us. I hoped he wouldn't hear my heart beating as I edged past. I was in a total fizz. Did they mean we would all sit at the same table? My stomach felt as if an octopus were inside.

Trimble's was filled with its usual wonderful smells of chocolate and caramel. Everything sparkled red and white with cute canopies over the side booths.

Danny led the way and Star looked over her shoulder at me and smiled. I wondered if anything this special would have happened if I hadn't been with Star. If I'd been with Janet? Janet might have grabbed the chance and made it happen. Janet is very good at grabbing chances. That's why she has so many conversations with Danny. I sometimes think she lies in wait for him and pounces.

Danny stepped back to let Star go in the booth first. What a gentleman! This had to be a first for Danny DePuzo. Star slid all the way to the wall. Quick as a flick Danny slithered in beside her. Quick as another flick, John squeezed himself in opposite her. I noticed how neither of them stood back for *me*.

But Mark was still waiting. My mind zipped around. Should I go next to John? I'd be opposite Danny. Or next to Danny? Oh, wow, that would put me vis-à-vis Mark. Or else right next to him. Either possibility took my breath away. As I debated, I remembered something from the book. "Never waste an opportunity. Seize the moment. It may not come again." This was a once-in-a-lifetime opportunity. I had to seize it right.

"C'mon, Karen, sit somewhere," Danny said.

I moved fast, in beside Danny. Mark sat opposite me.

Oh, heaven. Those were *his* hands on the table. I'd never been this close to him. Except once when he'd thrown me a volleyball on the playground. I blinked at his hands. No warts. No bitten nails. Total perfection.

His foot accidentally kicked my ankle. "Sorry," he said.

"That's OK," I muttered.

Danny looked from side to side, all smiles. "I could say I'm the cream in the Oreo cookie," he said.

"Or the baloney in the sandwich," Mark said, semi-sarcastically, and I laughed. I told you Mark's no dummy.

Danny was asking Star where she'd moved from and stuff like that. I wished Janet were there. It didn't seem fair that she was missing all this. If she'd been there we would have had a real lucky number . . . three boys and three girls.

Even though banana coconut was the flavor of the month, we all ordered chocolate, except Mark, who ordered strawberry.

"Don't you like chocolate?" I asked.

"I like strawberry better."

Instantly I decided to switch from a chocolate birthday cake to a strawberry one.

The malts came, all thick and frothy, the straws standing straight in them. There were long spoons on the side so we could get the last drop from each tall glass.

I took a sip and stared secretly at Mark. He had pink froth on his upper lip. On him it looked good.

"Hey, Karen?" John asked. "Did you ever find out about those traps?"

"Not really." I hoped John wasn't going to start questioning me about that again. But he'd gone back to talking to Star.

I wished and wished I could think of something to say to Mark. My mind was a total blank. Baseball? I knew a bit about baseball. The Dodgers? I'd ask him what he thought the Dodgers' chances were for a pennant win. And then I realized . . . HE was speaking to ME.

"I hear you're real good at tennis, Karen."

He'd heard I was good at tennis! Who had told him? Who cared?

I leaned forward, my eyes fixed on his face, my hands resting on the table. I should be modest, of course.

"Well," I began . . . and suddenly one of my two straws went up my nose.

In a sharp second I saw Mark's horrified stare

and I jerked my head back and pulled the straw out. Oh, let me die!

I sneezed and sneezed and sneezed again into my pretty red-and-white-striped napkin. Oh, just let me die!

And then, as if this weren't all terrible enough, John Hunt, the creep, gave a great big laugh.

"Did you guys see that?" he asked, real loud. "Karen's straw went up her nose! Do you always drink through your nose like that, Karen?"

I could have killed him.

"Are you OK?" Mark asked.

I wiped the tears from my eyes with my trusty napkin and tried to nod. The inside of my nose stung terribly.

I sneezed again.

"Sorry I missed it," Danny said, when I came up for air. "Do you want to do it again, Karen?"

I could have killed him too.

Star was leaning forward, looking at me around Danny. Star, who would never do anything as gross as sticking a straw up her nose.

"I bet it hurts," she said. "I got a pencil stuck in my nose once. It was awful."

"A pencil?" Danny was all interested. "How did you do that?"

"It was at my other school. I was chewing on the end of it. Someone behind thumped me on the back and the pencil slipped. I tried to pull it out but it had one of those big, wide erasers on the end. I had to go to the emergency hospital."

KAREN KEPPLEWHITE IS THE WORLD'S BEST KISSER

"Criminy." I could tell John was impressed.

"They had to use forceps."

"Stick with the straws, Karen," Danny advised. He really is a yuk.

I thought it was super-nice of Star to tell that awful thing about herself. If it had happened to me I'd never have told, not as long as I lived. I'd have to thank her afterwards.

I took a quick drink of the malt to revive myself. And then I remembered that one of the straws had been up my nose. Grosser and grosser.

Well, I'd had my once-in-a-lifetime chance with Mark. And I sure had blown it.

Chapter Seven

The boys walked us home. Actually, they said they'd walk us to Star's apartment building—which is, of course, where my Gran lives too. I said I was stopping in to see her. I hadn't planned to, but I did need to see Gran. Besides, wouldn't it be embarrassing if the boys all stayed there with Star, and I had to go the rest of the way by myself? Too humiliating!

Never in all my life would I have believed that walk home. There I was, strolling along Lake Avenue with Mark beside me. And I was miserable.

In front of us Danny and Star and John were tripping along, talking a mile a minute. Mark and I hadn't said one word. No, that's not true. Once Mark said, "Hi, Dennis" to some guy who passed on a bike. Once I said "Sorry" and then "Thanks" when I dropped my purse, and everything fell out, and Mark helped me pick it up. What next, I ask you? I'm not usually such a klutz. That dumb purse just somehow slipped off my shoulder.

All the while my nose throbbed like a time bomb about to explode. I tried to get a glimpse of it in store windows as we passed. But I couldn't see anything out of the ordinary, except me walking with Mark Ritchie.

When we reached the apartment house, wouldn't you know it? Gran was in the lobby, bringing in her evening *Star News*.

"Hello, Karen. Hello, Star."

As we said hello I thought Gran looked at me funny. She was probably wondering what that giant balloon thing was, growing out of my face. I put up my hand and touched it gently. Then I introduced them all. "This is my grandmother, Mrs. Kepplewhite. This is Danny, John . . . and Mark."

Gran's blue eyes never miss a thing. She knows all about these guys from my stories. Her look lingered longest on Mark.

"Nice to meet you," she said. "Do you want to come up and have some lemonade?"

Danny spoke quickly. "Uh, no thanks." I don't think Danny's too big on grandmothers.

"Are you coming, Karen? We could get in a half hour's cubing." Now I have to say something about my grandmother. She is very smart. Also, she knows me very well. She would *never, never* have taken me away from three boys, to sit with her and cube, except that she could tell, just by looking at me, that I needed to escape. That's how smart my Gran is.

"Sure." I pressed my Kleenex to my nose.

46

"Take care of the schnoz, Karen," Danny said.

Star smiled. "Thanks for coming with me, Karen."

I looked at Mark. "See you," he muttered.

But did he want to? Probably not.

Upstairs, in the safety of Gran's apartment, I told her all.

"Mark will never, ever look at me again, Gran. It's finished." I leaned my head on the arm of her couch, and heard myself, and felt a little silly . . . like stupid Julie in Gran's stupid soap opera.

"I didn't know it had ever started," Gran said mildly.

"It's over before it had a chance to begin," I whispered and giggled, and felt better.

We mulled it over, Gran and I. Gran is very good to mull with.

"I'm sure you're thinking about what happened more than they are," Gran said. "They've probably forgotten about it already."

She gave me some cream to put on my poor sore nose.

"Danny will never forget it," I said. "He's such a pain. I can't figure why Janet likes him."

Gran split the wax on our cube bags. "You can't? Poor little Janet just wants to be important to someone, that's all. She's settled on Danny."

"But why him?"

"Who knows? She probably has her reasons." Gran smiled. "Come on, baby. Let's cube."

Cubing is such an automatic thing. Your brain

47

turns and clicks one way while your fingers turn and click another. It doesn't stop you thinking.

"I know Mark was disgusted with me," I said at last. "He didn't talk to me at all on the way here."

"Did it ever occur to you that Mark may be shy too?"

"A *boy?* Shy? You've got to be kidding!"

Gran did one of her famous W. C. Fields impressions. "Now that's a sexist remark, little girl, if ever I heard one. I think I'll ship you off to Philadelphia."

Sometimes I'm not exactly sure what Gran's talking about.

She gave me some of her "tutti-frutti" salad to take home. It's just all kinds of fruit, layered in a jar, that melt together so you can't tell one kind from the other. It's heaven. Gran may not think she's a good cook. But she sure is good at putting things together and making them taste terrific.

She also gave me the tube of cream for my nose. "It doesn't look bad at all," she assured me. It's a fact of life. People who love you will even lie to make you feel better.

Later, after dinner, Janet came over.

Once again, I told my terrible tale. Janet was envious and horrified at the same time. She didn't know whether to say, You lucky! or You poor thing, so she said both.

"Wasn't that nice of Star, though?" I asked. "To tell that awful story about herself?"

Janet took off her tennies, sat on the floor and

pulled at her toes. "She's probably going to expect to be your *best friend* from now on."

For some reason I thought of Gran saying, "Janet needs to be important to someone."

"I have a best friend," I said. "But we could include her, I guess. She's really nice, Jan."

"There's *no such thing* as three best friends," Janet said. "One ALWAYS gets left out." She opened the book.

I sat with my chin in my hands. "Honestly, I don't know if it's worthwhile going on with this part of it. Mark's never going to want to kiss me. And I don't care if I get to be a terrific kisser, just for somebody else."

"Come on, Karen. You have to be ready if opportunity knocks."

Janet didn't understand. Opportunity had knocked already and I'd slammed the door on it.

" 'Body language,' " Janet read. " 'How to let him know you're interested.' "

We practiced body language. Janet sat in my chair and did stuff, and I had to guess what her body said. It was easy most of the time.

"Get closer," I said. "That's what you're saying."

"Right." To say get closer you put your hand where he can hold it if he wants to. It's very important to have it palm up. That means acceptance. Maybe if I'd put my hand palm up on the table in front of Mark today he'd have come closer. Then he could have gotten my other straw up *his* nose.

Janet and I practiced squeezing hands. She held mine and I held hers. Squeezing one way means, "I'm interested. How about a kiss?" It's tricky though. If you accidentally squeeze the wrong way it means, "OK, buddy. That's enough."

"I sure hope *they* know as much about squeezing as *we* do," Janet said. "We wouldn't want them to get the *wrong message.*"

We found out what to do if you meet *him* and you look tacky. You're supposed to smile and let your personality shine through. I decided the people who wrote this book don't know a thing about tackiness. I'd looked tacky today, all right. Try smiling with a straw hanging out of your nose.

"Tomorrow night's our LAST CHANCE," Janet said. "We've got to practice the *actual kissing.* There's no time left for messing around. And we'd better know it all. There's going to be BIG COMPETITION."

I knew she meant Star. She was right.

"I just wish we had someone to practice ON," Janet said. "I wonder if Wilmer would come over for you." Janet was talking about her stupid big brother. He cracks his knuckles all the time he's talking to you. Crack, crack, pop, pop, crack. Each one has its own special tone. It's really gross. Janet says Wilmer can't help it; he only does it because he's nervous. That's what the doctor told their mom. Maybe cracking his knuckles is his way of trying to be important.

"Wilmer would PROBABLY come if I paid him," Janet added.

I wanted to say, Not even if you paid *me*. But that would have been very rude. After all, he *is* her brother. "Better not ask," I said instead.

So next night we practiced on our own.

"I wish you had a DOG," Janet said. "A dog would be nice to kiss."

But we don't have a dog. So we practiced on our hands. What you do is make a fist and then you kiss in the place between your thumb and your curled-up fingers where it's sort of mouth-shaped.

"You're supposed to lick your lips to get a little shine," Janet said. "But not too much. We don't want to drip."

I shuddered. "Yuk. I've just thought of something. Wouldn't it be gross to kiss someone you didn't want to kiss? Maybe they'd have drippy lips."

"Don't think about things like that," Janet advised. "Anyway, all the boys coming to your party are cute."

I nodded. "Mark and John are, for sure. And Danny," I added, just to be nice.

"Michael Moss is kind of cute too," Janet said. "He has a fabulous back."

"Back?" Imagine noticing somebody's back! Honestly, Janet looks at the weirdest things.

She began to read again. " 'Breathe normally. If he's wearing glasses, try not to fog them up. That

51

will distract him from the business at hand . . . you. Practice, practice, practice.' "

"Easy for it to say." Janet picked up my Neddy Teddy from my bed and kissed him on his black stitched lips.

"I don't suppose your brother, Georgie, would let us practice on HIM," she suggested. "A real, live person would be great."

I rolled my eyes. "Are you kidding? A robot *does not kiss.*"

After we practiced some more we read the last-minute tips. Janet ticked them off on her fingers.

" 'Brush your teeth.

Use breath mints.

Rub bath oil into your hands.' " (That's for when you're running your fingers along his neck and telling him his hair smells nice. My stomach gurgled.)

Janet set the book on my bedside table. "Well, we've done all we can. Who'd ever have thought that this kissing stuff would be so complicated?"

"Tomorrow night's the test," I said. "The party."

Janet's face was a strange, pasty color. "Graduation," she said.

I wouldn't even let myself think that not everyone, always, graduates.

Chapter Eight

*E*verything was ready for my party.

I'd had my shower, shampooed my hair, and dressed in my new knickers outfit. It's pink, with a strawberry for the shirt pocket. That's just about where Mark's honey bear is on his shirt. Gran had bought the knickers set for my birthday and Mom and Dad had bought me pink Capezio shoes, almost like ballet slippers. I'd never had Capezios before.

My nose had a little pink swelling, that looked like a bump, about halfway up. Georgie had told me five minutes ago that it exactly matched my strawberry. I'd already been in the bathroom twice to dab it with "Cover All, covers every blemish." But this bump was no ordinary blemish.

The place cards were in place. Janet would be mad, but I'd put Star at the table for five, with us and Danny and Mark. Was it obvious, the way I'd put Mark right next to me? What would we talk about? Would I dare use some of that body language to show him I was interested? Maybe he'd know anyway, because of the place cards. Maybe he'd wish he were right next to Star instead of across from her. Maybe I should have put her at the other end of the room!

By now I was so nervous I wanted to throw up.

When the doorbell rang, Georgie ran to open it. A good thing too. I'd never have made it. He'd wanted to wear his space monster suit tonight, but Mom had explained that he'd scare everyone away. So he'd settled for Superman.

My first guest was Janet. We pressed sweaty palm to sweaty palm.

"Did you put the bath oil on your hands?" she asked.

I nodded.

"Me too. I think it just makes them slimy. Let's go quick and wash it off."

We examined one another in the bathroom. "Your *nose* doesn't look too great," Janet said. "No offense. But I LOVE your knickers. I'm dying to get some."

I hitched at mine. "I'm not sure if I should pull them up or down. Down, I look like a pirate."

Janet giggled. *"Up,* you look like a baseball player. I'm only kidding. They're DARLING. Leave them down." Janet brushed her hair. "I feel so OUT OF IT in a dress. Am I OK?"

"You look great."

"Did you remember to say *you-know-what* before you went to sleep last night?"

" 'Karen Kepplewhite is the world's best kisser.' I said it. Did you?"

"No, *I* said, 'Janet Hamm's the world's best kisser.' "

"Should we say it again now?" I asked. "I think my subconscious forgot already."

We stood, muttering. Then Janet opened her eyes. "How did you do the place cards?"

"I have you right next to Danny," I said.

"And where did you put Star?"

We froze as the doorbell rang. Our frightened eyes met in the bathroom mirror.

"We could stay in here all night," I whispered.

Janet gasped. "Are you *kidding?* Remember who's COMING?"

Superman was ushering in Francine Grady and Judy Bell.

Pretty soon Maria Guerrero came and then Connie Wu.

"Six girls," Francine said. "Trust the boys to be late."

"And *Star*," Janet said. "Hey! Maybe she *forgot*. Or decided to skip it."

They all had heard about Star from Janet and me. The thought that she might not come after all cheered everyone up.

Then the bell rang, and there she was.

"This is Star Sumner," I said. They knew, of course, but still I had to introduce her to all of them. Even though they were prepared, I could tell they were dazzled.

Star was wearing knickers, too, pale blue with a white ruffled shirt. Her shoes were white patent and she had a shoelace in her hair, tied on one side. The lace was white and covered with little blue flowers. We smiled at each other and I pulled my knickers up, like hers. I felt very with it.

"Here," Star said. "Happy birthday Karen." It was a Judy Blume diary, the kind that has no dates in it. You can write when you feel like it and if you don't feel like it, you don't have to write anything.

"Too bad she *has* one of those already," Janet said. "No offense."

"It doesn't matter," I told Star. "Because there are no dates I can keep it till next year. I'm hoping there'll be more happening to write about then. Anyway, I've only had awful things this year. Like straws. And you can bet I didn't write about that."

Star and I giggled and Janet giggled too and said, "Wasn't that the WORST?" I think she wants Star to know I tell her everything and that she's still my best friend.

"Well, let us in on the joke," Francine said and Janet said airily, "Oh, it's nothing, Francine. Simply nothing."

"You guys," I said. "I'm getting awfully nervous. What if none of the boys shows up?"

Everyone was suddenly quiet.

"Did they tell you they'd come for sure?" Connie asked at last.

"What EXACTLY did they say?"

56

And then the bell rang and Francine said, "Oh OH, here they are."

I knew we were all thinking "Oh OH" because it had to be the boys. I was so relieved and so scared at the same time that my knees were weak.

Janet gave me a shove. "So go open it, Karen!"

I went.

Chapter Nine

Danny and John came together, and I have to say John is very handsome. Not like Mark, of course, but pretty cute. They both brought me albums. I think boys think albums are good things to buy for girls.

After they'd wished me happy birthday, Danny made a rude remark about my strawberry. It was just the kind of thing you'd expect from someone interested in Fallopian tubes. He and John headed right for the table on the side where Mom had set out chips and dip and a big bowl of popcorn. They would! And then, with their hands full, and their mouths full, they strutted across to Star.

Janet gave me an I-told-you-so look. I guessed she'd be giving me a lot of those tonight. Wait till she found out Star was at our table!

I couldn't worry too much about Janet, though. I had worries of my own. Were John and Danny going to be the only boys? That would be awful!

Then three more arrived, all in a bunch. And wouldn't you know Mark would be last? But at least he was here. Here!

I tried not to stare at him. He was wearing a blue checkered shirt and dark blue corduroy pants and he looked adorable. His hair was wet, as if he'd just come out of the shower.

"I'm sorry I'm late," he said. "I had to wait for my dad to drive me."

It's amazing to think he has a mom and a dad just like ordinary people. I wondered if they were nice.

He gave me a square, deep box. "Happy birthday."

When I opened it there was a giant-sized Rubik's Cube. Someone must have told him about Gran and me and our competition. Star? Last night? And he'd remembered!

"It's called Rubik's Revenge. There are about a million possible combinations." I'd never noticed before what a gruff voice he has. So manly. Actually, I haven't heard his voice too often.

"A million combinations?" I said. "Gee." The book would really have been ashamed of me. Where was my brilliant conversation?

Mark was glancing around and in about two seconds he wandered away. I tried not to be suspicious, but I was, and when I looked, I saw that my suspicions were correct. Mark had drifted straight to Star. Maybe she was magnetic, like the North Pole.

Now that everyone was there we started the games. There was one where we split up into two teams and passed an apple from under our chins. The way it worked out, I had to take the apple from Mark. It only worked that way because I'd positioned myself correctly.

When Mark bent so I could reach his chin with mine, his breath was on my cheek. I guess mine was on his. Our noses brushed accidentally on the changeover and it was heaven, though I have to admit it hurt. I hoped my "Cover All, covers all blemishes" didn't move from *my* nose to *his*.

We played some more games, but unfortunately Mark and I didn't get to bump noses again. Then Mom called out that dinner was ready.

Janet and I exchanged meaningful glances. I hung back a little to let my guests go into the dining room ahead of me. After all, I am the hostess. Besides, I didn't want anything to be too obvious.

When I did go, I couldn't believe my eyes. Four boys had already helped themselves to food from the buffet. And they were all sitting at the same table. One of the boys was Mark. The others were Ferdy, Victor Simms, and Michael Moss. Oh, horrors! Hadn't they seen the place cards?

I looked at the tables, and I couldn't see them either. They'd disappeared. I stood, stunned.

Janet came rushing over to me. "Where are the cards?" she whispered, all aquiver. "Look what's happening."

"I can SEE what's happening," I hissed. "I'm not blind."

Star had seated herself at the table for five and just as I looked Danny and John grabbed the chairs on either side of her.

"Somebody took those cards," I said. "And you *know* who I suspect." I glared at Danny, who was so busy helping himself to a handful of carrot sticks from the bowl on the table that he didn't even see me.

Francine served herself fast and nabbed one of the two empty chairs left at that table. Trust Francine. She can always see what's going on and make the most of it.

"Oh, Karen." Janet sounded as if the end of the world had come. She was looking from the table with the four boys to the table with three girls, to the table with Star and Danny, and only one seat left.

I gave her a shove. "Quick. Get that empty chair next to Danny before one of the other girls goes for it."

"But it's *your* birthday."

"Go," I said. I really am a very good friend. Besides, and to be honest, I didn't want to sit next to Danny. If Mark had been there I'd have jumped hurdles to get that last place.

I wondered if I should try splitting Mark's group up in a joking sort of way. But they'd know I wasn't joking. And that would be too embarrassing. Should

61

I make a fuss and tell them about the cards? I didn't have the nerve.

Star called over, "Karen? Karen, would you rather sit here?" She half got up.

Janet was waving at me violently to come. *She* would have traded me for Star at Danny's table any day of the week. Danny and John pulled at Star's arms, frantic that she was getting away. It would have served them right if I had taken her place. But I didn't want to. That was not where my heart lay.

"Thanks anyway, Star. I'm fine here."

So there I was. On my very own birthday at a table with three other girls. Not that I don't like Maria and Connie and Judy. I do. It's just that they're not very different, compared to boys. I sat down and began to talk in an up way to show how perfectly happy I was. Judy and Connie and Maria were talking and gesturing very jazzily too, so we'd all know no one cared a bit. In fact, Maria was waving her arms around so vivaciously that almost the first thing she did was spill her grape juice.

"Sorry," she muttered.

Everyone was looking at our table. I wanted to say, "*I* didn't do it." It would be too awful if Mark thought I went around being klutzy *all* the time. But I didn't say anything. I just left to get some paper towels.

My family was munching away in the kitchen.

"How's it going?" Dad asked.

"You're not going to believe this." I jerked towels from the roll. "Danny DePuzo took all the place cards away. And four boys sat down at the same table. That means there are four girls at mine."

"See?" Georgie asked. "I knew they'd want it that way. You're so stupid, Karen."

I stared at him. "YOU?"

Georgie filled his mouth with salad so I could hardly hear what he was saying. But I heard.

"You'd made it so that the boys had to sit with all those dumb girls. Nobody'd want that, Karen. I fixed it for you."

He felt in the pocket under his cape and pulled out the cards.

"You . . . you . . ." Words bad enough wouldn't come.

Even Mom was shocked. "Georgie! You had no right to do that! This is Karen's party. I'm very, very angry with you."

"I'm telling you, Mom, Georgie's going to grow up to be another Danny DePuzo." I pointed a shaky finger at him. "And you needn't think you're going to get away with this, Georgie Kepplewhite. I'll get you. I swear I will!"

"Four boys at the same table." Dad grinned. "Those poor guys. They're nervous, kiddo. They're huddling together. I used to do that at parties when I was their age."

"*Those poor guys!*" I repeated sarcastically. "Gran and her 'shy'! You and your 'nervous'! They're just . . . just morons, that's all!"

Janet gave me another of her looks as I came back into the dining room. Face it, things were off to a not-so-great start for both of us.

I guess the food was pretty good. Everyone kept saying so, and going back for seconds. I'd been afraid one of the boys might try the kind of spaghetti stunt they sometimes pull in the cafeteria . . . dropping pieces down the girls' necks. Or sticking it in their hair. But they didn't.

Then Dad carried in the birthday cake, studded with strawberries and with all the candles lit. He put it in front of me and everyone gathered around. I looked up, secretly, to see where Mark was. Great heaven, he was right behind me! I hoped he could smell Mom's Arpege that I'd splashed behind my ears. I gave my head a little toss to waft the scent in his direction. Unfortunately when I tossed my head I saw that Star was behind me too. Had Mark come to stand behind me? Or beside her?

"Blow out the candles. Blow out the candles," Georgie chanted. His cape fluttered and his eyes glowed behind his mask.

I took a deep breath and heard Danny DePuzo say, "Careful, Karen. Don't get one of those candles up your nose."

I think I hate Danny DePuzo. He's such a turkey. It's pretty bad to hate the boy your best friend loves. But I hate Danny anyway.

And then, miracle of miracles, I heard Mark growl, "Shut up, will you, Danny."

Mark was defending *me*.

I took another deep breath, wished, and blew. Every candle went out. Oh, if they only knew what I'd wished for!

Gran and Georgie handed the cake around on paper plates. Someone sat down next to me. I didn't even have to look. My sixth sense told me it was Mark—sitting with *me* and not with Star.

"Good cake," he said at last.

"It's strawberry." Boy, I thought, I'm so witty and interesting somebody should put me on a talk show!

"Hey, Karen." Danny held a strawberry up on the end of his fork. "This matches your top." For a terrible moment I'd thought he was going to say it matched my nose. I was so grateful he hadn't that I actually smiled at him.

Some of the kids helped carry the dirty plates to the kitchen when we'd finished, and then we all stood around, looking at each other.

It was Danny, of course, who made the first move. "Is it time now for Spin the Bottle?" he asked in a baby kind of voice. "I just love Spin the Bottle."

His baby voice didn't fool anyone. Danny was anxious to get started on the serious stuff.

I swallowed, wanting it, not wanting it. "It's time," I said. What else could I say?

Chapter Ten

Janet and I sneaked out to the bathroom while the tables and chairs were being folded and put away. It's funny about leaving the room to go to the bathroom when there are boys around. You know it's natural, and that they have to go too. But somehow you don't even want them to see you heading in that direction.

The minute we got behind the closed bathroom door Janet asked, "What HAPPENED, Karen? I could have *died* when I saw that all the place cards were missing."

"Georgie," I said. "Can you believe he'd do that? But at least you did get to sit with Danny. I was stuck with all girls."

Janet sniffed. "Much *good* it did me! Danny and John were both KILLING themselves, trying to impress STAR. I smiled my *best* smiles at Danny and started up a *whole bunch* of really interesting conversations. He didn't even listen. And there was

Francine, all the time trying to get *John's* attention from Star. Why *did* you invite Francine anyway?"

"I told you. She invited me to her party."

Janet looked forlorn. "It doesn't matter. When a boy has his mind on Star, forget it. There's no way to unstick him."

We brushed our hair and cleaned our teeth. Janet had remembered to bring her toothbrush in her purse. She had brought her breath mints too, and we each sucked on one to be ready for THE BIG EVENT. I wondered if Mark's mind was on Star, too. I reminded myself that he had sat next to me at cake time and not next to Star. But still.

"I don't know why you like Danny anyway," I said, as I applied more Cover All to my bump. "He's such a toad. Did you hear what he said to me about the candles?"

Janet's eyes met mine in the mirror. "I know. It's just that . . . it would be really nice to have a boyfriend. And none of the other girls likes Danny."

I let my eyes slide from hers. "But why Danny?" I'd asked Gran. "She probably has her reasons," Gran had said.

Well, here was the reason. Janet thought Danny would be easy to get because no one liked him. What kind of a reason was that?

"Look," I began. But I knew she'd never listen to me. Especially not now.

Janet took a shaky breath. "Well, this is it. Kissing time. At least we're well prepared."

67

I nodded. Horrors! Horrors! Horrors!

When we opened the door I saw Star outside.

"Hey," I said. "You should have told us you were here. We'd have let you in."

"It's OK." Star smiled at Janet. "Thanks for telling me about the lettuce in my teeth. I'm just going to make sure I got it all out."

Janet peered at Star. "You got it."

"Star had lettuce stuck in her teeth?" I asked as soon as the door closed. "Star?" I couldn't believe anything like that would ever happen to Star. But, of course, she *had* once had an eraser in her nose.

"Yeah. I almost didn't tell her. Francine whispered to me not to. She said it would even things up for the rest of us if Star looked a little gross. Kind of like a handicap in golf, you know?"

I nodded.

"But what the heck?" Janet said. "It's so sneaky not to tell. And besides, if she had a whole salad stuck in her mouth she'd still be gorgeous."

We paused outside the door of the family room to swallow the last sliver of our mints. Then we breathed on each other. "Yours is nice," I said. "Pepperminty."

Janet sniffed at me. "Yours is nice too. I wonder, does it last long? I wish someone would invent something so you could check. Like a breath thermometer." We exchanged timid smiles and opened the door.

Everyone was sitting in a circle on the floor with

68

Danny in the middle. He was playing with an empty Coke bottle.

"Here come two of them," John said. "One still missing."

Yeah, I thought. The important one.

I let my eyes move around, looking secretly for Mark. There he was, over by the window, sitting on the rug like the guy on TV who teaches yoga.

Janet and I eased ourselves into the circle.

"Uh, uh. It has to be boy, girl, boy, girl," Danny ordered, and Janet moved. I wondered why Danny had been so quiet when I needed boy, girl, boy, girl at the table. Rotten old Danny.

"Why don't we just begin," Francine suggested. She would.

"No way. We're waiting for Star." Danny turned the bottle, always snatching it up before it stopped spinning.

"You'd think this was your party, Danny De-Puzo," Francine said. "You're so bossy! And anyway, it should be Karen who gets to spin the bottle first. It's her birthday."

"That's all right," I muttered. I shot a look at Mark—who seemed to be examining the pattern on our rug, tracing it with one finger.

"Go ahead, Karen," someone said.

"Yeah. Get out of the middle, Danny. You'll get your turn."

"OK, OK." Danny stood up.

"I don't want to be the one to start," I bleated. But Michael Moss was shoving me, so I went.

69

I sat looking at the bottle in front of me. If it had been a tarantula I couldn't have been more scared of it. Where was all this wonderful confidence the book had promised me? I was supposed to be superready.

"Here's Star." Danny patted the rug beside him. "I saved you a place."

"So start, Karen," John said. "Give it a good spin."

Oh, help. I put my hand on the bottle and closed my eyes. Let it stop on Mark. If it doesn't, I'll die. Don't let it stop on Mark. If it does, I'll double die.

"Spin, spin," everyone called. Didn't *they* feel the way *I* felt? Wasn't anyone else terrified?

I kept my eyes closed and spun.

I have to tell you about the way we play this game. When the bottle points at someone, you don't just rush over and give that person a peck on the cheek. It might be easier that way. What happens is, you both go outside in the hallway. Everyone inside begins to count out loud. When they get to sixty they shout "Time, time," and then you're supposed to come back in. We call it sixty seconds in heaven. With the wrong person, believe me, it can be sixty seconds in the other place. Maybe even with the right person.

Some parents don't like Spin the Bottle, but mine don't mind. They allow the hallway light to be dimmed, but not off. Mom says dim is more romantic. Gran says it helps because you can be sure you're kissing the right person. Dad says someone

70

could bump into something in the hallway and get hurt. Georgie says the whole thing is dumb. None of their reasons fool me, but I like the light on myself. Who knows what might happen in the dark?

My parents also plan on being right there, about six feet away in the kitchen with the door open. I guess if someone screamed for help they'd peel out into the hallway, ready for action. It's nice to know they don't object. It's also nice to know they're close by. I don't know why that's so nice, but it is.

All of these things were going through my mind as the bottle spun and I sat there with my eyes squinched shut. Sixty seconds in heaven were hanging in the balance. And wouldn't you know it pointed right at Star? When a girl stops on a girl, of course, you have to spin again.

"I'll trade your turn for mine," John said quickly and laughed to show he was kidding.

Star laughed too and got pink.

"No fair," Francine yelled, and Danny said, "John knows that's not in the rules. Spin again, Karen."

What agony!

This time I had no strength left and the bottle just curved once, then stopped. Pointing right at toady old Danny DePuzo!

Danny immediately jumped up.

I glanced desperately at Mark, who was still studying our rug. I never knew that rug was so interesting. I swung my gaze to Janet, who gave me one of her familiar sorrowful looks. Boy, I'd have

71

traded with her happily. I'd have traded with anyone.

"Come on," Danny smirked. "Sixty seconds in heaven."

As I walked past Janet I whispered, "Count fast, OK?"

Danny and I stood facing each other in the hall. Maybe he wouldn't want to kiss me? Fat chance! Danny doesn't believe in wasting anything.

"You're not going to burp on me this time, are you?" Danny pretended to be ready to run. I wished he would.

"I would if I could," I told him. "Would you like to skip the kissing part? I won't tell if you won't."

"Oh, no you don't. Don't try to weasel out of it." Probably he wanted a chance to practice for Star. I needed practice too. It was still early. And Danny might be better than my hand or Neddy Teddy. At least he was a person. A semi-person. I closed my eyes and concentrated. First, lick your lips. I licked.

And then I saw Danny licking his lips. Yuk! Maybe we'd slide off.

He took my hand and ran his fingers up the inside of my arm.

I stood, frozen. What *was* this?

Danny put his arms around me. I tried to let myself melt against him, the way the book advised. But it's harder when you're really doing it. I didn't feel one bit melty. Suddenly, I felt Danny rubbing my neck at the back. "Your hair smells so nice," he whispered. "And it's so soft."

And then . . . unbelievable . . . I felt him kiss my ear.

I gave him a shove. "Danny DePuzo, you big fake! *You* read the book."

Even in the dim light of the hallway I could see how red his face was. "What book? I don't know what you're talking about."

"You do too. You stood there in front of the window of Brown's Book Store and you said all those mean things about Mary Lou and Betsy Sanchez, and how anyone would be dumb to buy the book and even dumber to read it." I stopped for breath. "And then you sneaked right in there . . ."

"Forty-eight, forty-nine, fifty," came the voices from inside.

Danny looked at the door, all guilty, scared to death that someone had heard. "Sh! Sh!" he begged.

"Sh, yourself." I tried not to giggle . . . imagining Danny DePuzo, the great lover, lying in bed practicing from the book just the way Janet and I had done. Maybe even kissing his hand, or his teddy bear. Or his baseball! Oh, crumbs!

"Time, time," came the chant from inside.

"You're not going to tell anyone, are you, Karen?"

The giggle slipped out. "I won't tell." Once Danny got over the shock he'd figure out that I must

73

have read the book too. How else would I have known? But he wouldn't dare tell on me either.

He opened the door for me and smirked his way into the middle of the ring. What a put-on! I couldn't get over how sure of himself he was. Poor Janet could hardly bear to look at me. If she only knew! I wondered if I couldn't just tell her.

"That was great," Danny said. "Now, who's next for sixty seconds in heaven?"

Janet sat forward, her eyes glued on the blur of brown glass. But Danny got Connie.

Connie looked all flustered when she came back in. Probably that book stuff works real well if you don't know where it comes from. That's what I was hoping anyway.

Connie spun next and got John Hunt, and John got Star.

"Hey!" Danny yelled. "Spin that bottle again, John. You didn't do it right."

John grinned. "I did too."

We had to call "Time" twice, and then Danny had to go and bang on the door before John and Star came back. Star's hair was all messed up. I wondered if John could have read the book too. How weird that Danny and John might think they had to. They talked as if they knew everything—and as if they'd done everything too. I had a feeling Star liked John. If he got her for a girlfriend, I bet he'd stop biting his nails.

Star spun then, and I had my fingers crossed that

she wouldn't get Mark. Not Mark, please. She got Michael, and Michael got Janet.

Janet gave me one of her bursting-to-tell-you looks when she came back. Janet has quite a selection of different looks.

I tried to imagine what had happened. Had Janet done her expert kissing on Michael and had he fainted at her feet? Had she run her fingers through his hair? Whatever, they both looked awfully pleased with themselves.

And then, wouldn't you know it, Janet got Mark. Mark! I tried to smile at them as they went past. Have you ever seen a camel smile? It looks as if it's in pain. I'm sure I was smiling just like a camel. I have to say Mark didn't look too thrilled either.

They came back before we counted to thirty. Great! It couldn't have been too wonderful. And now Mark was in the middle and my heart was going skippity-skip again.

He spun the bottle and it whirled as if it would never stop. I was going cross-eyed trying to keep track of it. Was he hoping it would be Star?

Stop bottle, go bottle, stop! Can you will an inanimate object to do what you want it to? Well, there's the guy who can bend spoons just by looking at them. I was trying.

The bottle skidded, slowed, and stopped. On me! Oh, horrors! Oh, heaven! Me and Mark, Mark and me. What if he was disappointed?

"No fair," Francine squealed. "Karen's had

sixty seconds in heaven already. Somebody else should get a turn."

"It's Karen's birthday," Janet said. "There aren't any rules for her. And who put you in charge, Francine? No offense."

Janet is a really true friend.

"Yeah, let Karen go," Danny added. "She can use the practice."

At any other time I would have come up with a smart and snappy instant comeback. But my brain wasn't working. Nor was the rest of me.

It was all I could do to stand and stagger to the door that Mark was holding open for me. It was all I could do to whisper to myself, "Karen Kepplewhite is the world's best kisser."

Chapter Eleven

I didn't dare look at Mark as I sidled past him. What if he were yawning? Or looking back longingly at Star? Stop it, Karen, I told myself. Be confident.

We stood, facing each other in the dim hallway. There was a space between us, big as a tennis court. If we'd had a couple of rackets we could have volleyed.

I tried frantically to remember something from the book. This was certainly no time to giggle or to ask Mark what school he went to. The octopus was awake again in my stomach.

"Twelve, thirteen, fourteen," came the chant from inside.

Mark didn't move. Did the book tell you what to do if the boy didn't move? I couldn't remember.

From the kitchen I heard the theme music from *M*A*S*H*. I wished I were in there watching with Mom and Dad and Gran and Georgie. But how could I want that when I was here, out in the almost dark, with beautiful, wonderful Mark?

"Nineteen, twenty, twenty-one."

Almost half of my heaven time was over and nothing had happened. Was he waiting for me to start?

His voice made me jump. "You don't want to . . . kiss . . . do you?"

What did he mean, I didn't want to kiss? Oh, crumbs! I gave a fake, tinkly laugh. "I don't care." What a lie. But how could I say, "Yes, please?"

"Well . . . I know you don't *like* to kiss . . ." Pause, pause.

This couldn't be happening. He knew I didn't want to kiss? Didn't like to kiss? And after I'd been practicing all week. After I'd learned to kiss expertly, soulfully, sexily, just for him?

Beyond Mark I saw a small, shadowy movement. It was Georgie.

"Mom! Dad! Georgie's looking," I yelled.

"There's nothing to see," Georgie yelled back and disappeared. It was all too humiliating.

"Danny told me," Mark said.

My heart reeled. "Danny told you?" I was coming on like a total space cadet.

"Forty-five, forty-six, forty-seven . . ."

"That you didn't like kissing. That for sure you wouldn't be having any kissing games at your party. That's why . . ." He stopped.

But I knew the end of the sentence. That's why he'd come. *He* didn't like kissing. Rotten old Danny had told Janet that Mark was coming because of the kissing games. He hadn't bothered to say he was coming because he thought there wouldn't be any.

"Fifty-eight, fifty-nine, sixty."

"TIME! TIME! TIME!" The chant came through the door like cannibal drums through the jungle.

"Well, I guess we'd better go in," Mark said.

He opened the door for me.

Mark has very nice manners.

I couldn't help wondering what would have happened if it had been Star out there with him instead of me. Was it just certain people that he didn't like to kiss? Certain people with ugly bumps on their noses?

Janet raised her eyebrows at me as I sat back down in the circle. I was too miserable to pretend a smile. It was my turn again to spin the bottle. But I was too miserable even to do that.

"I've had my chance," I said. "I'll give to Francine." I thought the words sounded super-sad. *"I've had my chance."* They didn't sound sad to Francine. She was in the middle of the circle with her hand on the bottle before I could even blink.

I guess the party went on. Kids went out to the hallway and came back in. Everyone seemed to be having a good time. Nobody cared about me. After all, I was only the birthday girl. I wasn't important. I told myself I didn't want Mark anymore. Who'd want a boy who didn't like to kiss? What did you do instead of kissing?

We were supposed to play Truth or Dare next,

79

and Janet and I had set up a little plan. If she got to ask me, I'd say "Dare." Then she'd tell me to go out for sixty seconds of heaven with the boy of my choice. I would do the same for her. But who cared, now? Well, Janet did, for one. And everyone else seemed to also.

We stayed in the circle on the floor.

"You're first," Francine said to me. "You get to ask the first Truth or Dare."

I should say that we also have our own rules about Truth or Dare. If the person chooses "Truth" you can't ask what boy or girl that person likes. Anything else *has* to be answered and no chickening out ever. With "Dare," you have to do whatever you're dared, unless it could get you into trouble.

Mostly everyone picks "Dare." If you can't tell who you love, the truth part isn't so interesting. With dares there's always kissing and stuff.

"Truth or Dare, Janet?" I asked.

"Dare."

"I dare you to take a boy out for sixty seconds in heaven."

Janet gave a very cute and feminine giggle. It was definitely the kind the book guaranteed would turn a guy on. I was glad at least *she* was happy.

Danny was already scrambling to his feet.

"Michael Moss," Janet said.

I couldn't believe it. She'd chosen Michael over Danny. They must have had a good time all right in Spin the Bottle. Maybe Janet and Michael were going to start liking each other, which would be great. Michael's a lot nicer than mean old Danny DePuzo. He probably has a nicer back too.

Janet and Michael disappeared and we began counting. I looked at Mark, sitting on my floor, in my room, in my house, and the wonder of it all swept over me. He had the nicest arms, fuzzy, but not furry. Maybe they'd get furry later. I hoped not. Oh, Mark. I felt all choked up. I was going to cry! Criminy, what for? Maybe Mom's right that thirteen is a weepy age. I don't think I like thirteen—I don't think I like it at all.

I looked at Mark, all swimmy and blurry, and suddenly I realized something scary but wonderful. I could be out in the hallway with him again.

Although I was jumpy and anxious now, I was thinking hard. Maybe that's part of being thirteen too. I couldn't help noticing that Danny hardly ever got picked for anything, in spite of his wonderful bod. Francine didn't get chosen much either, and she was definitely the prettiest girl there, except for Star. I figured that was because Danny and Francine were mean a lot of the time.

I honestly believed Star would have been taken for every turn if it hadn't been against the rules. But I didn't think it was only because she was gorgeous. It was because she was gorgeous *and* nice.

Those were all interesting thoughts. But right then I was more interested in seeing if I would get out into the hall again with Mark.

That lucky Connie! She got the next turn and now she was asking Mark "Truth or Dare." I could hardly stand it.

"Truth," Mark said.

"Truth?" Almost no one ever says "Truth." I guess Mark chose it because he doesn't like to kiss. Well, I was glad about that now, at least.

Connie had a hard time knowing what to ask him.

"Is it true that you once held Francine's hand behind the girl's gym?" she asked and giggled.

"Connie!" Francine was mad but Connie pretended not to see.

I sat forward in horror. *Had* he? Had he held Francine's hand behind the girl's gym?

"No," Mark said.

And then the total miracle happened.

"Truth or Dare, Karen?" Mark asked.

My heart was choking me.

"Dare," I whispered.

"I dare you to come in the hallway with me." Mark's face was as pink as my strawberry.

It had happened! It really had happened.

"Me?" I pointed to my chest, then quickly let my hand slide down to a less noticeable part of my anatomy. Actually my chest is the least noticeable part of my anatomy, unfortunately.

"Yes." Mark doesn't mess around with words.

I hoped he wouldn't see Janet nodding and giving me a great, happy grin. How embarrassing!

"We're counting already," Danny warned. "Hurry it up. I want another turn."

And the rats really *were* counting already. "Six, seven, eight" came echoing after us as Mark closed us together in the romantic gloom of the hallway.

Everything was unreal to me. Maybe I was in a state of shock. I'd never been in shock before but this could easily be it. Mark had picked ME. A little voice inside my head asked . . . why? Why? And another little voice begged, "Help, somebody. Help!"

"Twelve, thirteen, fourteen." I could hear Janet inside, trailing one beat behind all the others, trying to slow them down. Good, true Janet.

Mark was leaning against the wall farthest from me, not talking, not moving, not even looking at me. Didn't he realize that our heaven time was disappearing fast? Or maybe heaven time wasn't what he had in mind. Then suddenly he was speaking.

"Have you figured out how to solve the cube yet?"

"What?"

"The Rubik's Cube. The regular one."

He'd brought me out here to talk about the cube! My heart sank.

"No," I said.

"Twenty-one, twenty-two, twenty-three."

What if I rushed at him, grabbed him, and pressed my lips firmly to his, tilting my head so our noses didn't bump? What if I put my arms around his neck and let my fingers linger? . . . I coughed. Of course, I couldn't. It was all very well for the book to tell you to seize the moment, but some moments aren't easy to seize. My hands were wet, and it wasn't from bath oil. I licked my lips, not in preparation for anything, but because they were dry as dead leaves.

"Have you read the book?" Mark asked.

I stared. "The book?" Oh, no! He'd read the book too. The whole world and its circling planets had read this book!

"The book on how to do it." Mark sounded a little desperate. "It tells you exactly how."

I swallowed. "I know."

"Thirty-four, thirty-five, thirty-six."

"I haven't actually read it myself," Mark said. "But a friend of mine did."

"I know," I said again. Danny, of course. I thought I might be dying.

"It always seems so easy till you try it." Mark scratched his head. Even in my frozen state I noticed that he looked very attractive when he was scratching his head. Just as attractive as when he was scratching under his arm.

"I know." I seemed to know everything.

"You just have to line everything up. Make sure all the sides match."

I nodded. Put that way it sounded a little strange.

"Forty-one, forty-two, forty-three."

"Once you've read the book I guess it's really hard to go wrong. I hear you're pretty good."

He'd heard I was pretty good! Karen Kepplewhite is the world's best kisser, I reminded myself frantically, and I spoke before I could lose my

84

poor, shivering courage. "That's because I've read the book too. Do you want me to show you how to do it?"

Maybe he *knew* I'd read the book before he asked me out here. Maybe Danny had managed to whisper it to him. Maybe he wanted a demonstration from an expert.

"You mean now?" Mark sounded a little amazed, I had to admit.

"If you like." This was really embarrassing. When I write to the book people I might tell them about this as a sort of case history.

"Fifty-two, fifty-three, fifty-four."

"We probably don't have time," Mark said. It's funny, I could tell he was getting his courage up too. Could he really be shy, like Gran said? And nervous? Just as nervous as I was. Nobody ever said boys could be shy and nervous, except Gran and Dad, but I guess they can be.

"It wouldn't take long," I muttered, but even to myself I didn't sound too sure.

"TIME! TIME! TIME!" came the triumphant shout from inside.

Mark leaped from the wall as if someone had shoved him from behind.

"Karen? I didn't mean to talk about books on how to solve the cube. I don't even really care." His words came so fast that they fell over each other. But I heard them all right.

"Books on . . ." Oh, good grief! That's what he'd meant. Not kissing, or stroking, or nibbling, or any of that stuff. There *were* other books in the world. I'd just forgotten. Had I given myself away? What had I said? I'd never, never . . . Through the babble of my thoughts I suddenly heard what he was saying:

"I *really* wanted to ask if you would play tennis with me on Saturday. We could go for a malt after."

His feet were shuffle, shuffle, shuffling on the rug. He *was* nervous. He was scared too. Inside the family room my friends sounded like a bunch of angry bees.

"Will you, Karen?"

"Yes," I said. There truly are times when you don't need all that interesting conversation stuff, and this just happened to be one of them.

"You will? Whew!" Mark pretended to wipe his forehead the way you do when something's a big relief. He smiled. It was a shaky, unsure smile but it still turned me to mush. He was happy! And it was me he'd asked, not Star, not anyone else. Oh, Mark!

And then, awesome beyond awesome, he leaned forward and his lips bumped against mine. A kiss! It was so fast that I couldn't believe it had happened. But I knew it had. For a moment I thought I might faint or something, but of course I didn't.

He opened the door real fast and I stumbled into the den. Mark's face was still red. I'm sure mine was too. Everybody would know we'd kissed. How wonderful!

Janet was beaming at me. So was Star. And I was beaming at everyone. My first kiss. My first date. My first real, live experience with a boy!

You know what? If this is what's it's like to be thirteen, I think the whole year is going to be terrific.

ABOUT THE AUTHOR

EVE BUNTING was born and went to school in Ireland. She moved to California in 1958.

Mrs. Bunting began writing in 1969 and has written more than a hundred books for children and young adults, many of which have won awards. Besides *Karen Kepplewhite Is the World's Best Kisser,* her books *Ghost Behind Me* and *Strange Things Happen in the Woods* are available as Archway Paperbacks.

One day while browsing in a bookstore, Eve Bunting found a book that gave instructions on how to kiss like an expert. Paying for it at the checkout stand was a little embarrassing, but, as she told the clerk, "Who doesn't need to learn more about an important subject like this?" Having learned more, Mrs. Bunting felt qualified to write *Karen Kepplewhite Is the World's Best Kisser!*

Mrs. Bunting and her husband now live in Pasadena, California. They have three grown children.